Barney's
Sing-along Stories

BINGO

Written by Gayla Amaral
Illustrated by Darren McKee

SCHOLASTIC INC.
New York   Toronto   London   Auckland   Sydney
Mexico City   New Delhi   Hong Kong   Buenos Aires

Farmer Barney had a dog
And Bingo was his name, oh.

And Bingo was his name, oh.

Farmer Barney had a dog
And Bingo was his name, oh.

MEOW-I-N-G-O
MEOW-I-N-G-O
MEOW-I-N-G-O

And Bingo was his name, oh.

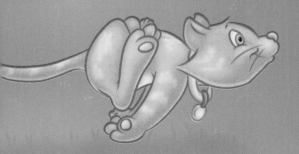

Farmer Barney had a dog
And Bingo was his name, oh.

MEOW-RIBBIT-N-G-O
MEOW-RIBBIT-N-G-O
MEOW-RIBBIT-N-G-O

And Bingo was his name, oh.

Farmer Barney had a dog
And Bingo was his name, oh.

MEOW-RIBBIT-QUACK-G-O
MEOW-RIBBIT-QUACK-G-O
MEOW-RIBBIT-QUACK-G-O

And Bingo was his name, oh.

Farmer Barney had a dog
And Bingo was his name, oh.

MEOW-RIBBIT-QUACK-OINK-O
MEOW-RIBBIT-QUACK-OINK-O
MEOW-RIBBIT-QUACK-OINK-O

And Bingo was his name, oh.

Farmer Barney had a dog
And Bingo was his name, oh.

To: BINGO
From: Barney

And Bingo was his name, oh.

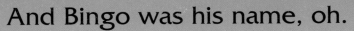
And Bingo was his name, oh.